My Spiritual Alphabet Book

Holly Bea
Illustrated by Kim Howard

H J Kramer
Starseed Press
Tiburon, California

Art Directors: Linda Kramer and Assumpta Curry
Design: Assumpta Curry, Tiburon, California

Library of Congress Cataloging-in-Publication Data
Bea, Holly, 1956-
My spiritual alphabet book / Holly Bea ; illustrated by Kim Howard.
p. cm.
Summary: Rhyming verses introduce the letters of the alphabet and the concepts of God as Creator, Mother Earth, self-esteem, and joy.
ISBN 0-915811-83-9
1. Children—Religious life. 2. English language—Alphabet—Juvenile literature. [1. God. 2. Conduct of life. 3. Self-esteem. 4. Alphabet.] I. Howard, Kim, ill. II. Title.
BL625.5.B43 1999
291.4'32—dc21 98-32194
CIP
AC

H J Kramer Inc
Starseed Press
P.O. Box 1082
Tiburon, CA 94920
Printed in Singapore
10 9 8 7 6 5 4 3 2 1

For my wonderful parents
and my newest nephew, Aidan.
H. B.

For the generous educators
of our tender children.
K. H.

Aa

A is for the Angel
Who is watching over me.

Bb

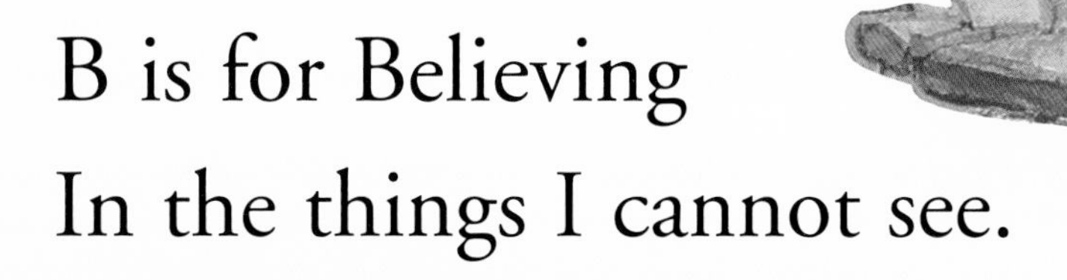

B is for Believing
In the things I cannot see.

Cc

C is for our Creator,
Who made the world so fair.

Dd

D is for the Dance of joy
And happiness we share.

Ee

E is for Everything God has made,
From big to very small.

Ff

F is for my loving Friends,
Who help me when I call.

Gg

G is for the Grace of God
That fills me every day.

Hh

H, it stands for Heaven—
It's where the angels play.

Ii

I is for the Inspiration
That helps me reach the stars.

Jj

J is for the Journey
That will take me oh-so-far.

Kk

K is for the Kingdom
God created at the start.

Ll

L is for the Light of God
That lives within my heart.

Mm

M is for our Mother Earth,
With trees and oceans blue.

Nn

N is for the starry Night,
When wishes can come true.

Oo

O is for the Olive branch
That's carried by a dove.

Pp

P is for the daily Prayer
I send to God with love.

Qq

Q is for the Questions
I will ask along the way.

Rr

R is for Remembering
The beauty of today.

S is for the Spirit
That fills my heart with joy.

Tt

T is for the Truth I tell
To every girl and boy.

Uu

U is for the Universe
God made for me and you.

Vv

V is for the inner Voice
That guides the things I do.

Ww

W is for the Wisdom
That tells me wrong from right.

Xx

X is in the eXtra hug
I get from Mom at night.

Yy

Y is a letter that I love
Because it stands for Yes!

Yes! to love and Yes! to health
And Yes! to happiness!

Zz

Now we're at the very end;
We're at the letter Z.

You find it in amaZing,
Which is what I am, you see!

This is my special alphabet—
God made it just for me.
So when I count my blessings,
I can use my ABCs.